THE FOOL

Rachel McLean writes thrillers that make your pulse race and your brain tick. Originally a self-publishing sensation, she has sold millions of copies digitally, with massive success in the UK, and a growing reach internationally. She is the author of the Dorset Crime novels and the spin-off McBride & Tanner series and Cumbria Crime series. In 2021, she won the Kindle Storyteller Award with *The Corfe Castle Murders* and her books regularly hit No 1 in the Bookstat ebook chart on launch.

Joel Hames is a Lancashire-based writer of crime fiction, and the editor of million-selling books across multiple genres. Joel's own works include the Dead North series featuring lawyer Sam Williams, and the psychological thriller *The Lies I Tell*. Most recently, he has been working with titan of crime fiction Rachel McLean on the hugely successful Cumbria Crime series.

ALSO BY RACHEL MCLEAN AND JOEL HAMES

Cumbria Crime series

RACHEL
McLEAN
& JOEL HAMES

CUMBRIA CRIME NOVELLA

THE POOL

ACKROYD
PUBLISHING

Ackroyd Publishing

ackroydpublishing.com

Printed and bound by CPI Group (UK) Ltd, Croydon, CR0 4YY

CHAPTER ONE

Trixie Burns stood above the pools at Tongue Pot, watching Eileen and Ada splashing below. Joe stood to one side, his eyes on Ada.

Ada knew that Joe was only here for her. She was wearing a modest one-piece, but given the way Joe stared at her, Trixie reckoned she'd have drawn his attention in a plastic bag.

Joe wasn't a bad lad. But Ada could do better. And the fact that Joe and Ada were still here, rather than off somewhere private, like Liam and Bella, suggested that Ada *knew* she could do better.

Nearby, Gregory Howgill stood alone, silent, his arms folded. If it weren't for the scowl on his face, Trixie would have assumed he was admiring the view.

But Gregory Howgill didn't admire anything. Why he even bothered with these walks was beyond her.

If she was braver, she'd ask him. Maybe suggest he find another group. But Trixie wasn't built for confrontation. Probably why she worked with animals instead of people.

That left Liam, Bella, and Pete. Pete had wanted to see Lingcove Beck Falls and the hidden cave waterfall, and he was old enough and experienced enough to find that himself. Liam and Bella had wanted privacy and pressed on to Esk Falls. Trixie had given them her spare map.

It was a beautiful day, one of those rare, glorious May mornings. In the still waters of the pools, a blue, cloudless sky shone back at her.

She glanced at her watch. The walk had been straightforward enough, but the ground was boggy in places. And the weather could turn fast up here. Visiting Hardknott Pass any time, except on a day like today, and it would be a lot less hospitable.

Probably time to gather her flock and head back to the car park.

"We'll need to go soon," she called out. Eileen looked up and nodded, saying something to Ada. Eileen spent her working days and nights dealing with drunks at the Miner's Yard. If anyone could get young Ada moving, Eileen could.

Trixie turned and began to walk away, the noise behind her receding. The mountains loomed on all sides, giving the illusion of solitude.

She hadn't made it to the stone bridge before she saw Liam and Bella. Walking quietly arm-in-arm towards her. Beads of water glistened in their hair, the very picture of young love.

She couldn't help liking these two. Bella was a teacher, or training to be one. Liam worked at the Port. Not an obvious pairing. But seeing them together, she knew. That generation hopped from partner to partner like – well, like rabbits, really. But she had the feeling these two would stick together.

She smiled. "Time to head back."

They nodded and walked back towards the others. Just Pete to go.

She pressed on, up the dirt path to the bridge. She could hear the cascade of Lingcove Beck Falls.

"Pete!" she called, turning her head left and right. There was no sign of him on the rocks that formed its rim. She took another few steps, and looked down, at its base.

Just a glance. She didn't expect to see Pete there, because it was a tiny plunge pool, not as still as the others. Beautiful to look at, but for a swim, she'd pick Tongue Pot or the holes beyond, the ones Liam and Bella had been exploring.

But there he was, floating in the water.

"Pete!" she called again.

He didn't move.

Odd. The water was loud, but so was Trixie, when she wanted to be.

"Pete!" she shouted, louder this time. She began to descend the rocks to the pool, moving carefully.

Still no reply. Still no movement. As she reached the pool, her voice began to falter.

She took a step towards him. She hadn't been able to make it out from above, but from here it was clear.

Pete was floating face-down, bobbing in the tiny pool. She took another step, reached out a hand, pulled it back again, took a breath.

She had to do this.

She touched him. Cold.

But of course he was cold. The water was freezing, even on a hot early summer's day. The water here was always freezing.

"Pete?" she said, her voice catching. She blinked, swallowed, and reached forward with both hands to turn him over.

His eyes were open. Staring blankly at the sky.

Trixie had seen enough bodies in her time. Usually four-legged rather than two, but the same principles applied. If they weren't breathing, they were usually dead.

And Pete Whiteside was quite definitely dead.

CHAPTER TWO

"Have you heard from Olivia lately?" Aaron asked.

DI Zoe Finch paused. "No."

She'd heard from David Randle, though. Former Chief Superintendent David Randle, hiding out somewhere in Cumbria with Olivia. Aaron didn't know Randle had rescued Olivia, brought her up here, and got himself shot in the process. Zoe couldn't help feeling conflicted about that gunshot. A few inches to one side, and she'd never have had to worry about David Randle again. As it was, she had to listen to him whingeing about his injured hand.

"But she's around, yes? She's in Cumbria?" Aaron pressed.

"Last I heard." Zoe shook her head as she pushed open the door to the team room. Aaron didn't know about Randle, but Nina and Tom didn't even know about Olivia. Or at least, they didn't know she was back.

If she was back. What use was her being in Cumbria if she wouldn't come out of hiding?

"Boss," said Nina and Tom.

"Anything come in?" Zoe asked.

"Nope," said Tom.

"Then I trust you're busy with the books," she said to Nina. The DC looked away.

"Nina?" Zoe said.

"Boss?"

"Don't play dumb, Nina. When's the exam?"

"Not till next month."

"Eighteen days," added Tom.

Nina shot him a look that made Zoe wince.

"What will your mum say if you fail?" asked Tom.

Beside Zoe, Aaron cleared his throat. "Any news on the IOPC report, boss?"

He knew there was no news on the IOPC report. Whatever it was they were looking for, it would be months before anyone knew whether they'd found it.

Zoe was about to tell him as much when her phone rang.

She glanced at the display. Dr Robertson. What was the pathologist calling her for? She didn't have any live cases with him.

"Chris," she said. "What can I do for you?"

"I've got something that might interest you," he said. "Suspected drowning the other day at Lingcove Beck Falls. One of the pools up by Tongue Pot."

"Tongue Pot?"

"It's a beauty spot near the Hardknott Pass."

Christ. The place names up here.

"Hang on." She put the speaker on. "I'm with the team. Suspected drowning, you say?"

"That's right. Day before yesterday. Looked like an accident, but I've just done the PM, and I'm not so sure."

"Why not?" asked Aaron.

"Well, first off, because the man didn't drown."

There was a short silence. Zoe looked around the room, waiting.

"How did he die then?" said Nina.

"Head injury. Consistent with an irregular blunt object."

"Like a rock?" asked Tom.

"Could be," the pathologist replied.

"I've been up round there." Tom frowned. "Lingcove Beck. It's quite steep. Couldn't he have just fallen and bashed his head?"

"Yes, but if he had, there'd be similar damage to other parts of his body. Contusions from the fall, cuts, bruises, little scrapes. But apart from the injuries to his head, Pete White-side was a perfectly healthy twenty-eight-year-old male. You know it's not my job to make these calls, DI Finch, but unless a rock somehow fell from a height and landed perfectly on the man's head, I'm all but certain he was killed."

Zoe's attention was drawn by the sound of tapping: Tom's fingers on his keyboard, moving fast, bringing up the report from the incident, which appeared a moment later on the big screen.

"Any signs of struggle?" Zoe asked.

"You mean skin under the nails, that kind of thing? Sadly not. Anyway, I've sent the PM report to your team inbox, Zoe. But there's always the chance of extracting someone else's DNA, if you can tell me where to look for it. Anyway, I have to go. Let me know if you have any questions."

"OK. Thanks." Zoe turned to the screen, which now included a summary from the pathologist's report in one corner. There had been eight people on the walk, an informal group based in West Cumbria who'd met on social media and had occasional outings to the Lake District under the guidance of one Trixie Burns.

"I know Trixie," said Tom, breaking the silence. "She's a vet. Took care of my mum's cat."

"When you say 'took care of...'" said Nina.

"Yes, but that doesn't mean... I mean, it's her job. Just because she..."

Nina laughed.

Tom picked up the plastic coffee cup from his desk and threw it at her. "Next time it won't be empty," he said.

Zoe carried on reading. Eight names. The dead man had been a heating engineer. Besides him, there was the vet, a teacher, a consultant, a nail technician, a barmaid, a port worker, and a man whose occupation had been described by the uniformed officer who'd attended the scene as 'unclear'.

Zoe's attention was drawn to the port worker. Liam Cunliffe. A familiar name. Hadn't he been on Bobby Silver's old shift? But Nina was looking elsewhere.

"Bloody hell," she said. "Look, Tom. Eileen was there."

"Eileen Carmichael," he read, blank-faced for a moment before his expression cleared. "Oh. Eileen Carmichael. From the Miner's Yard."

Yes. That was a name Zoe had seen before. She'd been interviewed in the course of the karaoke bar investigation. The Patrick Hutchinson murder.

"Good," Zoe said. "Well, we've got names, and it looks like we've got contact details and workplaces, too. Let's go visit these people. Ask for prints and DNA."

"Why?" asked Tom. "We don't have anything to compare them to."

"Not yet, no. But you never know. And it's useful to

judge someone's reaction. See how worried they are. Ask a few questions. Shake a few trees. See what falls out. I'll leave you to divide things up, Aaron."

CHAPTER THREE

AARON PARKED outside the Burns Veterinary Practice, got out of the car, and looked around.

It was a pretty spot, just back from the sea opposite Parton Village Hall. The waves were audible, the sky so huge and bright he'd be forgiven for thinking it had never rained here.

Trixie Burns was 'with a patient', as the receptionist, a girl who looked too young to be out of school, explained. She gestured towards a closed door, behind which Aaron could hear voices, one male, one female.

Presumably the patient's owner, rather than the patient.

Both owner and patient – a tortoise, or turtle, Aaron wasn't sure which – left a few minutes later, and Trixie Burns emerged.

Aaron explained who he was, and she ushered him through to her consulting room, a tiny, windowless space, all linoleum and metal. There were two plastic chairs, but Aaron had the sense that the humans in here spent most of their time either standing or crouching.

"It was awful," Trixie began. "Pete was a lovely man, y'know?"

"Did you know him well?"

She paused, her brow furrowed. "No. I suppose not. None of us know each other all that well. Apart from Liam and Bella."

He raised an eyebrow.

"They're a couple," she explained. "But the group – it's not been so long. A year or so. We've been out maybe ten, twelve times. Not everyone, every time. There are the occasional little tensions. Like Joe, fawning over Ada, when she's... Well, I don't think she's interested. But really, everyone seems to get along well. Apart from..."

She looked down.

"Apart from who?" asked Aaron.

"I shouldn't really... I mean, it's just, it's not illegal, is it, being, well, a bit... How can I put it?"

Briefly, thought Aaron. He waited.

"Gregory Howgill," she said, finally. "Management consultant. He doesn't seem to like anyone, just walks about scowling. He clearly doesn't enjoy it. Not sure why he even bothers."

Aaron spent the next few minutes pressing for more detail. Trixie had detail, but better than that, she had photos.

"I always take a few shots. For the Facebook page."

She sent him what she had, sixty photos, which was a lot more than 'a few'.

"It was all completely normal," she said. "Until... Well, you know. Pete said he wanted to see Lingcove Beck. Bella and Liam went to Esk Falls, bit of privacy." She shot a grin of complicity at him, and he smiled back. "The rest of us stayed around Tongue Pot, but not the whole time. People wandered off. It was a lovely day, you know?"

Trixie Burns said that a lot, 'you know?' He nodded. Sometimes it was better to say nothing.

"We just strolled about and enjoyed it. There was some swimming, some walking. I don't... Why are you involved?" she asked, fixing him with an appraising look, which reminded him that people didn't get to be vets if they weren't smart.

"We're just looking into it," he replied. "Just making sure everything is as it should be."

"What does that mean, precisely?"

Now it was Aaron's turn to flounder. "We're trying to establish the precise circumstances of Mr Whiteside's death," he said, simply.

"Detective Sergeant Aaron Keyes," she said, more to herself than to him. "I've read that name. You've been in the *Chronicle*, haven't you?"

He shrugged.

"You. Your team. You solve murders. Is that what you think? That Pete was *murdered*?"

There was an incredulity in that last word. He could hardly blame her. The sun, the sky, those photos. It was all so pretty. So straightforward. So much easier to imagine a tragic accident.

"That's what we're trying to establish," he said, attempting to regain control. "Now, would you mind providing me with a sample of your DNA? And your finger-prints. Just for the purposes of elimination."

Trixie Burns had no problem with that. "Do you have a weapon, then? Or something else to test?"

Smart, he reminded himself. "I'm not at liberty to say," he told her. She didn't seem satisfied with that, but it would have to do.

CHAPTER FOUR

Joe Kirkham moved slowly, scratching his head and staring in confusion at Nina. At first she wondered if he was ill, or stupid, or both. Then he reached past her for the kettle, and Nina smelled it.

Joe Kirkham was drunk. Still drunk from whatever he'd been on the night before. Possibly also stupid, or ill, or both. But definitely drunk. There was something in the way he moved that reminded her of something else, or someone else, but she couldn't place it.

"Yeah," he said, sitting on his bed with a coffee. He'd spilled milk on his t-shirt, and his trousers were unbuttoned and slipped down every time he moved, revealing pasty skin and a grey strip of boxer short that probably wasn't supposed to be that colour. He took a sip, belched, and looked her up and down. "So you're a cop, are you?"

"I am. Detective Constable Nina Kapoor," she said. Repeated. For the fourth time in the ten minutes she'd been in Joe Kirkham's tiny ground-floor studio flat in Corkickle. She swept her gaze across the place: unmade bed in the corner, pizza boxes and empty lager cans piled up by the sink. He followed her gaze.

"Not bad, is it?" He sat forward. "Fuck knows how I'm gonna manage this month's rent, mind. Hey, don't suppose you—"

"What's your occupation, Mr Kirkham?" Nina asked, forestalling the inevitable. He looked disappointed.

"Bit of this, bit of that."

"Unemployed, then?"

"For now, yeah. Not a crime, is it?"

"Not at all. Can you tell me about the trip to Tongue Pot, the day before yesterday?"

He nodded. "So this is about that fella. Pete. Right?"

He hadn't even asked what she was there for, when she'd knocked and he'd opened the door. Maybe he was used to the police dropping round unannounced. Or maybe it was just that he was still drunk.

"Yes. We're looking into—"

"Yeah, don't care," he interrupted. "It were just a day out, weren't it? Nothing special. Don't really know them, the others. Just Ada."

"That's Ada Malone?"

"Yeah. Thought I had a chance there. Turned out..." He shook his head, then looked her in the eyes. Something passed across his face; he was drunker than she'd thought. "Hey. Don't suppose you—"

"Really, Mr Kirkham?"

She raised her eyebrows.

Without looking away, he shrugged. "Can't blame a bloke for trying."

"Tongue Pot," she reminded him.

"Yeah. Look, a bit of a walk. Ada and the old bird went

for a swim. And that couple buggered off. Quiet shag behind a rock somewhere, I reckon. Pete buggered off, too. Probably spying on them."

Nina looked up from her notes.

"Why would you think that?"

He shrugged again.

"Dunno, really. Why not?"

"Did you have any reason to suspect Pete Whiteside of spying on them? Bella and Liam, isn't it?"

"Yeah, that's them. Look, it were just a... A thingy. A comment, like. Didn't mean anything by it. He weren't bad, Pete. Can't say I knew the bloke, but it's a shame he's dead. Owe him one, really."

"Why's that?"

"Well, it were a bust, weren't it? I were wasting my time with Ada, and if he hadn't died, I'd probably still be wasting it. But after that... I straight out asked her, didn't I? Thought, y'know, death and that, gets the juices going, thought I might have a better chance. Turned out I was wrong. Pete dying saved me a few more trips out to the fucking lakes."

Joe Kirkham knew almost nothing, and what he did know was no help. He agreed to provide prints and a DNA sample. Nina was surprised they weren't already on file, but then, she'd met wasters who weren't also convicted criminals before. Only a handful of times, it was true. But they existed.

And Joe Kirkham was one of them.

CHAPTER FIVE

BELLA FRITHSDEN WAS a tall Black woman with blonde streaks in her hair. She greeted Tom's appearance at her school with horror.

"You can't," she said, then blinked. "I can't talk to you." She turned and looked longingly at the line of children outside a glass door. "I can't."

"Why not?"

"Not here."

They were in the tarmacked playground outside the brand-new Woodville Primary School, a stone's throw from the old Marchon Chemical Works where Bernard Dearborn had been murdered nearly a year and a half ago. The new coal mine that they'd been hoping to put there wasn't happening now, but that wouldn't bring Bernard back to life. And it was getting to the point where Tom could identify bits of his home town from the bodies they'd found there. Bernard at Marchon. Daria at the marina. Huz in his own bloody house.

"I just want to talk to you for a minute, Ms Frithsden," he said. "It won't take long."

"It's Miss," she said. "No. That would be weird. That's what the kids call me. It's Bella. Look, I'm not really a teacher, you know?"

That was new. Had she lied to the uniform who'd taken her details? Or had there just been a mistake? He tilted his head, and she followed him a few steps away from the railings separating the school from the pavement. A group of parents, ostensibly there to watch their offspring enter the school building, seemed to be showing an undue interest in the conversation between him and Bella Frithsden.

"What do you mean, not a teacher?" he asked.

"I'm only a trainee. I can't bring the police into school. I need to finish this placement, detective."

Tom looked past her to see two mothers and a father openly staring at them. *What would they be thinking? An argument between lovers?* He had a girlfriend, of course, Harriett Barnes. They'd started to talk about moving in together, not that anyone here would know a thing about that. But Bella had a boyfriend, Liam from the Port, and if schools were still the same hotbeds of gossip they'd been in his day, every child and parent would know that.

"It won't take long, Bella. If we can just find somewhere to talk for five, maybe ten minutes."

She turned to look at the children, still queuing, then at her watch, then back at the children. She stared at them for a moment, then seemed to make a decision.

"Wait here." She took off into the building, past the children, leaving him alone and being watched by a group of parents that had now swollen to eight. He turned and looked back at them. Not one of them looked away. Not one of them even blinked.

Bella Frithsden was back a few minutes later, during which time the group had grown to eleven silent watchers, or almost silent; every now and then, one would turn and whisper something in a neighbour's ear.

"Come with me."

He followed her through the glass door, into the school, where the brightness of the morning was muted and a sense of calm pervaded, despite the background hum of young voices. She led him down a short corridor to a door, which she pushed open to reveal a room that was little more than a broom cupboard.

"The break-out room." She smiled. "I've managed to get one of the TAs to cover for a few minutes, but if the head finds out... Just, please, can we be quick?"

"Of course." He smiled. "I'd just like to know about what happened the day before yesterday. With Pete Whiteside."

Her mouth fell open.

"What?" he said.

"I thought... I assumed that was just an accident."

Only now did he realise that Bella Frithsden had an accent. Southern. Soft, but there.

"We're still looking into—"

"Oh my God." Her voice was low, calm, almost, but her eyes darted around, looking for somewhere safe to land.

"Listen to me," he said. "Listen, Bella. We don't know what happened to Pete. We're just trying to gather information. All I want is—"

"I just thought..."

"Bella." Her eyes came to rest on his. "Just tell me what you remember. From that day. And what you knew of Pete."

She nodded, sharply.

"It was a normal day. Up till... till Trixie found him. It was bright. The walk was easy. It's beautiful up there. Have you been?"

Tom nodded. Slowly, she was beginning to relax.

"We hung around. All of us. Then Liam and I went off. Trixie gave us a map. We went to Esk Falls. Had a little swim. Just the two of us."

"Was Pete with the rest of the group when you left?"

She frowned, then nodded. "Yes. I think so." Her frown deepened. "No. I'm sure of it. That was the last time we saw him. He was still with the group. We went off. Trixie didn't find him till after we joined up with everyone else."

So far, so unproductive. But it tallied with the reports from the scene, at least. He asked her to confirm she'd been with Liam the whole time, and she nodded. He asked her about Pete, but she'd only been in Cumbria eight months. She didn't know him well.

"He seemed like a nice enough man," she said, and burst into tears.

Tom waited. She reached into her bag for a box of tissues, swallowed, and calmed herself.

"Sorry," she said.

"Do you mind if we take a sample of your DNA? And prints?" he asked.

"Why?"

"Just for good order. We don't actually have anything to compare them with."

He smiled, and she nodded. He felt a little guilty for not adding "yet".

When he emerged after another ten minutes, there were

still four parents by the railings. He could still feel their gaze boring into his back ten minutes and two miles later.

CHAPTER SIX

ZOE CRESTED the rise to see Stella Berry standing ahead of her, arms on hips. Zoe had felt the bonnet of Stella's car as she walked past it in the car park at Hardknott Pass. It had still been warm.

"I hear you still haven't charged him," Stella said.

Zoe glanced around, but Stella was alone. Pity. With no civilians around to upset, this would have been the perfect crime scene for Keisha Middleton to investigate. Just Stella, Zoe, the blue skies, the rolling hills, and the tumbling beauty of Lingcove Beck.

"You mean Streeting?"

"Who else?"

Ralph Streeting had been arrested in January. He'd killed Bobby Silver, they knew that. They had the evidence. They even had the gun. But Ralph's case was complicated, what with him being a detective inspector, what with his arrest being part of something bigger, centred around Myron Carter's criminal enterprise at the Port of Workington.

"It's out of my hands," Zoe said.

"Tell that to Denise."

Denise Gaskill had been injured in the operation to recover that gun. She'd barely survived. Stella had been there when it happened, and she wasn't the sort to forgive and forget.

"Even PSD can't get near Streeting at the moment," Zoe said. "We certainly can't. For all we know, he's been charged with half the crimes in Cumbria. He must have been charged with something. But he hasn't been talking. If he had, Carter would be in custody. What have you got for me?"

Stella didn't move.

"What?" asked Zoe.

"How's Denise?" Stella shot back.

"Improving, last I heard. Go and see her yourself. What have you got for me?"

Stella nodded.

"Fuck all," Stella said. She pointed down, past the rocks, at the water. "Too many people. You see the tape across the footpath?"

"Yes. I'd have thought that would have kept people away."

"I put that there. Just now. No one thought this was a murder, remember? There were people walking away when I got here. Probably a load more yesterday. And what are we hoping to find?"

Zoe shrugged. "A murder weapon?"

"Chris Robertson tells me you're looking for a rock. Take your pick."

Stella gestured towards the pool. They could gather up all the rocks here, test them, spend years, maybe find the one that had been used to kill Pete Whiteside.

"So what, we're just wasting our time here?" Zoe asked.

"Gets me out of the office," Stella replied, this time giving an actual smile.

Zoe tried to smile back.

They'd poisoned this place for her, Streeting and Carter. And even if she put them both away, she wasn't sure it would ever feel clean again.

CHAPTER SEVEN

Tom had read Aaron's note on his conversation with Trixie Burns, so he wasn't surprised by Gregory Howgill. He stood outside the man's office for fifteen minutes while Howgill finished what he insisted was an important call. The door wasn't soundproofed, so Tom could hear nothing other than the sound of a man slurping coffee and playing on his phone.

After fifteen minutes, Howgill opened the door and gestured him inside. He sat behind a large wooden desk and pointed to a chair opposite.

"Well?"

He was a short man with wiry grey hair, metal-framed glasses, and a prominent nose in a face dominated by a scowl that didn't shift the whole time Tom was with him.

The whole three minutes.

"I was hoping you could tell me about the incident the other day. The death of Pete Whiteside. Any observations about the day, anything you've seen. Anything you know about the victim."

"I spoke to a policeman at the time."

A local PC had attended. Tom didn't recognise the name, but they'd done a good job, particularly given there was nothing suspicious at the time. Names, addresses, contact details, all on file. A decent description of the scene.

"We're just following up on that. We're interested in whether anyone wandered off by themselves, at any point. We know Liam Cunliffe and Bella Frithsden went off together. But if anyone else—"

"Why does it matter?" asked Howgill.

"The circumstances of Mr Whiteside's death aren't as straightforward as they seemed at the time. We need to make sure there isn't anything more to it."

"You mean he was murdered?"

Tom shrugged.

"Well, I didn't do it," said Howgill. "Hardly knew the bloke."

Tom waited.

"Look, I'm a busy man," Howgill said, lifting his arm and eyeing his watch. "Whiteside's dead, it was an unfortunate accident, and I don't have time to waste, Constable. I'm a busy man. If you want to speak to me—"

"Would you mind providing DNA and fingerprint samples, for elimination purposes?" Tom asked.

"Yes, I would mind." Howgill stood, walked around the desk, and opened the door. "If you want to speak to me, go through the proper channels. Until then, I'll consider this matter closed."

He waved at the door. Tom stood and left. *Was the man a murderer or just a shit?*

Ada Malone, by contrast, was more than willing to talk.

Tom found her scrolling on her phone and tapping her fingers on a table in the otherwise deserted nail salon she worked in. She was tall, botoxed, and bottle-blonde, and so perfectly groomed that it was hard to believe he was talking to a real person. Then she opened her mouth and started talking and the illusion fell away.

"Bloody hell. It's true then, is it?"

"What?"

"Pete. He didn't just fall. Pushed, was he?"

"We're not sure at the moment, Miss Malone."

"Christ, call me Ada. So, what, you're looking for motives, are you? Spoken to his wife?"

Aaron was on his way to speak to the widow. No one else had mentioned the woman so far. Tom looked again at Ada Malone and wondered if she wasn't as stupid as she looked.

"It's in hand."

Ada nodded. "Good. Well, Gregory Howgill don't like anyone, so he could have done it. Rest of us, we all got on fine with Pete. Seemed a straight-up guy."

This tallied with what everyone else had been saying, with the exception of Howgill, who hadn't really said anything.

"You spoken to Joe?" she asked, her lips pursed. Everything about her face seemed exaggerated, and Tom wondered if that was habit, or something forced on her by the surgery.

"One of my colleagues has," he replied.

"Right. Well, you see him, you tell him from me, I'm not interested."

Tom grinned. He'd read Nina's notes on her little chat with Joe Kirkham. "I understand he's got the message already."

Unlike Howgill, Ada Malone was happy to provide DNA and prints. Of course, they still didn't have anything to compare them to. The boss had messaged just before Tom went in: no sign of a murder weapon, no evidence at the scene.

Maybe Dr Robertson was wrong. Maybe it had just been an unfortunate accident. A fall, an unlucky landing. Tom couldn't help hoping that was what had happened.

Because if it wasn't, Pete Whiteside's killer was out there somewhere, and Tom had no idea how to find them.

CHAPTER EIGHT

HELENA WHITESIDE WAS THIRTY, short and muscular. Even though the semi-detached house in Egremont she'd shared with the late Pete Whiteside was normal-sized, Aaron felt the urge to shrink into the walls, like the place wasn't big enough for both of them.

They sat in the living room, drinking tea. Helena wasn't unusually wide, but she exuded a disproportionate presence. Quiet, not tearful, not distraught, as far as Aaron could see.

"Are you okay, Mrs Whiteside?"

She laughed, without mirth. "My husband's just died. What do you reckon?"

"I'm sorry," he began.

She held up a hand. "No. Don't be. That was rude of me. I'm sorry. Look, what do you want to know?"

He'd called on his way over. It was one thing to surprise a witness, quite another to spring a visit on a widow, even if they did turn out to be a killer, more often than not.

"We just want to establish all the details, Mrs Whiteside." He smiled. She didn't smile back.

"Is there something more to this?" she asked.

The checks he'd run before leaving the Hub had come back while he was talking to Trixie Burns. There was, as expected, a life insurance policy, with Helena as the sole beneficiary. But the payout was ten thousand pounds. For some people, more than enough to justify murder. For Helena, he thought not.

She ran a graphic design business, operating from home, with more than thirty thousand pounds in turnover each year for the last three years. He couldn't rule out the possibility that Helena had killed her husband. But if she had, it wasn't for the insurance money.

"That's what we're trying to find out," he replied. "Can you tell me where you were the day before yesterday, while your husband was on the trip to Tongue Pot?"

"So there is something more to this." She continued before he could comment, "Well, I was here. Working. You can check my documents, I suppose, but I was on the laptop, so it won't prove anything. Maybe you can do something clever with IP addresses."

They were the sort of words that would usually be accompanied by a smile, but there was no smile on her face.

Time to come clean.

"Do you know of anyone who might have wanted to harm Pete?" Aaron asked. He watched her face. No surprise. Confirmation of what she'd already suspected, maybe. But her fit, twenty-eight-year-old husband had just died, and there was a detective sergeant in her house. It was no great leap to the conclusion that Pete had been murdered.

"No." Her mouth remained open, as if she had something else to add.

Aaron waited.

"Would you like another cup of tea?" she asked after a few seconds.

"Mrs Whiteside, is there anything else that you think might help us? We're investigating your husband's death. If you can—"

"I was going to leave him."

The words left her in a rush, out in half a breath. It took him a moment to digest them.

"You were?"

She nodded.

"May I ask why?"

She shrugged. "He wasn't as nice as everyone made out."

Aaron waited, a beat, then two, but she didn't elaborate.

"Was Pete violent?" he asked.

She shook her head. "Oh, no. He wasn't violent, and before you ask, he wasn't controlling or gaslighting or any of that, either. Nothing sinister. He was just a bit of a selfish prick. You know, like most men."

There was a challenge in her look. Aaron wasn't going to take her on.

"Was there another woman involved?" he asked.

"Not that I know of."

"And this behaviour of his, do you think he might have made any enemies? If he was, as you say, a selfish prick?"

"No. Look, he wasn't a *bad* man. Not bad enough for someone to hate him. Just not good enough for me to want to spend the rest of my life with. He gave off this impression, like he couldn't do enough for me. And it was bullshit."

Aaron took a moment before he asked the next question. The obvious one.

"Did Pete know you were going to leave him?"

She shook her head. "Not as far as I'm aware, no. It's not

like I've done loads of planning. I'd just had enough. And no," she added, the challenge back in her voice, "there wasn't another bloke, either. I'm sorry Pete's dead. Like I say, he wasn't a bad man. But I'd fallen out of love with him a while ago. If anyone wanted to hurt him, then I've got no idea why."

CHAPTER NINE

AFTER JOE KIRKHAM, Nina's interview with Eileen Carmichael had been straightforward but brief. Eileen knew nothing about what had happened that day, and next to nothing about Pete Whiteside.

"I was in the water most of the time." She leaned past Nina to wipe a smudge off one of the Miner's Yard's old brass light fittings.

Cheryl Mosterkant was at the corner table, nursing what Nina imagined was the first of many gin and tonics. Eileen had turned the music up a fraction. Even Cheryl wouldn't be able to hear what they were saying.

"You spend much time up there?" Nina asked.

Eileen nodded, looking serious. "It's my me-time. I spend all my working life with this rabble." She gestured towards the customers, which at the moment comprised the orange-haired Cheryl and nobody else. "Need something better than that. So I walk and swim whenever I can."

Eileen's DNA and prints were already on file from the Patrick Hutchinson investigation. She'd have helped if she could, Nina was sure of it. The fact that she hadn't helped meant she really knew nothing at all.

Nothing at all was what she expected from Liam Cunliffe, too, but for a few minutes it looked like she wasn't even going to get that.

"Sorry," said the man who controlled the barrier that guarded the entrance to the Port of Workington. "I get where you're coming from, but I've just spoken to his shift manager, and he's busy."

"Busy?"

The man nodded and shrugged. He hadn't tried to help. Nina had heard him shouting into his walkie talkie that "the lad didn't have to talk to the pigs if he didn't want to."

It was shaping up to be another hot day, and the kiosk didn't offer much shelter. The man would be getting burnt later. By the look of him, he'd already been burnt, many times over.

Nina didn't feel the least bit sorry for him.

"Who's his shift manager?" she asked.

"Miles Stringer," he replied.

The name meant something to her. She picked up her phone, made a call, and waited in her car, blocking the entrance to the Port, for the person she'd called to make another call. The man in the kiosk stared at her while she waited, then gestured for her to move.

She ignored him.

Five minutes later, she heard his walkie talkie crackle into life. After a minute, the barrier lifted.

"Keep going," said the man in the kiosk. "Fourth turning on the right. They're waiting for you."

Nina had met Miles Stringer briefly during the initial stages of the Bobby Silver murder investigation. He'd been a friend of Bobby's, and had inherited the management of her shift. He'd also been an acquaintance of Aaron's, and it was Aaron she'd called. Clearly, he still had enough influence with Bobby's old friends to change a mind or two.

Not that it mattered. Liam, an anxious twenty-something with the sort of long wavy dark hair that would have had Nina weak at the knees a decade ago, was willing to help. Willing to provide prints and DNA. Willing to talk, too, as long as he had Miles with him. Miles kept checking his watch, but he needn't have bothered: everything Liam knew came out within a few minutes.

Yes, he'd been there. Yes, he'd wandered off with Bella, had left Pete behind with the rest of the group, hadn't seen him afterwards. Yes, he'd been with Bella the whole time. And yes, Pete had been nice enough, which was what everyone seemed to say about him, although what he was nice enough for was never made clear.

Liam hadn't chatted much with the other walkers. Truth was, he confided, he wasn't really one for the outdoors. "Get enough of that here, don't I?" he said, grinning as he turned to look at Miles, who smiled fondly back.

"Why are you in the walking group, then?" Nina asked him.

"Bella, she likes it. And if she wants to do it, I'll do it. It's not that bad."

A quiet, nervous lad, but clearly a keeper.

"Mind you," he continued, "it'll probably shut, now."

"What will?" Nina asked.

"The group. Not gonna want to carry on after someone's died, are they?"

Beside him, Miles shook his head. "Bloody hell, lad. If we had that attitude here, there'd be no one left to work."

CHAPTER TEN

AARON SAT IN HIS SKODA. Helena Whiteside's house in his rearview mirror. He dictated a summary of his conversation with her into his phone to upload to the team inbox. He'd looked through the updates from the DI, Nina, and Tom. Maybe Dr Robertson had made a rare mistake.

No one had disliked Pete Whiteside enough to kill him. As far as Aaron could tell, there wasn't even a financial motive. And every person on that trip to the pools, every person who might have been close enough to kill him, had been with someone else.

The couple, perhaps. Or some of the others.

But why?

He finished dictating his notes, turned the key, and glanced in the rearview mirror again.

There was a car there, outside Helena's house. It hadn't been there a moment earlier. A black BMW X5, tinted windows.

Illegal plates.

Two men got out of the front seats and sauntered up the path to Helena's front door.

Aaron got out of the Skoda and stood at the end of the path. The men hammered on the door.

Helena wasn't stupid. She wouldn't open it.

The door opened. Helena's face appeared in the gap. "Detective," she said, her voice drying up.

Shit. She'd thought it was him, returning for more questions.

"Whiteside?" asked one of the men.

"Can I help you?" said Aaron.

The men turned. Their identical crew cuts, the way their identical t-shirts bulged with the same muscles, their height, the way they walked. They radiated menace.

"Who are you?" the man said.

"Shut the door," said Aaron.

Helena nodded and shut it.

The men stepped towards him, matching stride for stride.

Aaron took a step towards them. He enjoyed the identical looks of surprise on their large, round faces.

One of them looked like his nose had been recently broken.

"Detective Sergeant Aaron Keyes," he said. "Can I help you?"

The men turned towards each other. They turned back to him.

"We're after Pete Whiteside," said the second man. "He around?"

"Why?"

"We've come to collect what he owes."

"Pete's dead, I'm afraid. Any issues, I suggest you take it up with his estate."

"This is his house though, right?" said the first man. Even their voices were identical.

Aaron said nothing.

"I hope he was a better saver than he was a gambler," said the other.

They walked towards Aaron. For a moment it seemed like they were about to walk right through him, but they parted and walked either side of him, then came together again as he turned to watch them.

"Why?" he asked.

"Because the late Pete Whiteside owes a lot of money," said the first man.

"Guess we'll 'take it up with his estate'," said the second, turning to Aaron with a smirk before he climbed into the driver's seat of the BMW.

Aaron watched them drive away, then knocked on the door. When Helena opened it, she had the chain on.

Over more tea, Helena admitted she'd known nothing of Pete's gambling.

Aaron had seen her reaction when she'd opened the door and realised it wasn't him banging on it. She hadn't expected anything like this, ever.

"I'll stick around for a bit," he said, picking up his phone to update the DI.

CHAPTER ELEVEN

WITH THE TEAM OUT, Zoe had planned to catch up on paperwork. She wanted to talk to Fiona. The Super had been out of sorts for months, since the IOPC investigation had kicked off. She wanted to call Randle, not that he'd answer, but she had to keep trying. She wanted to call Carl, too, and find out if he'd heard anything about Streeting.

But events were conspiring against her.

She'd barely stepped outside her office, on the way up to see Fiona, when she bumped into Alan Markin shuffling past, looking like he hadn't slept in days. After twenty seconds of excruciating small talk with her fellow DI, she felt her phone vibrating and looked down with relief to see Aaron calling.

She retreated to her office to hear all about Pete Whiteside's gambling debts and the gentlemen who seemed keen to collect. Then she called Nina to get her over to Helena's house. She could keep the widow company and study for her bloody sergeants' exam at the same time.

What would Aaron do, if and when Nina made

sergeant? He'd make a good DI – he'd acted up enough times over the years. Really, she should be encouraging him. Sure, she'd be losing a great team member. But it would be selfish to hang on to him if it meant holding his career back.

She stepped outside her office, checking the corridor was clear before heading towards the stairwell and Fiona's office.

Her phone rang again. Stella Berry.

"Stella? Don't tell me you've found the murder rock?"

"Not likely, no. But I've got something almost as interesting."

Zoe turned and walked back to her office.

"What?"

"Your murder victim. Pete Whiteside."

"He's not as squeaky-clean as we were led to believe," Zoe replied. "Gambling debts. Wife about to leave him."

"That's not the half of it. He's not actually Pete White-side, either."

Zoe fell into her chair, frowning.

"What?"

"Well, the man was identified, right? By the people at the scene, and then by his widow at the mortuary. We all knew who he was. Prints get taken, matter of course, but it wasn't like there was any doubt."

"Are you telling me there is doubt after all?"

Zoe reached out for the cup on her desk, then realised it was empty. She hadn't had the chance to grab a coffee since early morning, and now there was a blurriness to the afternoon that probably owed as much to tiredness as it did to whatever nonsense Stella was bamboozling her with.

Or maybe she'd caught something during that twenty-second conversation with Alan Markin.

"More than doubt," Stella replied. "And it's only luck I saw it."

"Saw what?" Zoe asked. It made a change. It was usually Stella getting worked up and everyone else trying to keep her calm.

"Calm down," Stella told her. "I just happened to flick through the folder for the case, just wanted to make sure we hadn't missed anything obvious, and it turned out we've missed something obvious."

"And that obvious thing is?"

"Pete Whiteside's prints belong to a man called Richard Black."

CHAPTER TWELVE

Nina knocked gently. The last thing Helena Whiteside needed was someone else pounding on her front door. The sarge let her in and ushered her through to a neat living room. A woman sat on a sofa, a glass and a bottle of whisky on the coffee table in front of her.

"Helena, this is my colleague, DC Nina Kapoor," he said. "This is Helena Whiteside. We've just had an interesting call from the boss, and Helena's explaining a few things to me."

"I'm sorry," said Helena. There was a catch in her voice, and a vulnerability to her. Nina frowned.

"Helena's just moved onto the whisky," the sarge said. "It's been tea up to now."

"Right," said Nina.

"Do you mind if I have a quick chat with my colleague outside?" he asked.

Helena paused in the act of tipping whisky down her throat and nodded.

In the kitchen, the sarge filled Nina in.

"Pete wasn't Pete," he said.

"What?"

"Not originally. He was born Richard Black. Changed his name nine years ago, after a short spell in prison."

"Bloody hell. So much for Mister Nice Guy. What was he inside for?"

"Death by dangerous driving. Stupid teenage accident, in Brighton."

"And she knew?"

"She only found out recently. That's what she says, anyway. You've read my notes?"

Nina nodded.

"So you know she was planning on leaving him. She says the fact that he'd kept this hidden from her all those years was the last straw."

"You don't believe her?"

He shrugged. "I don't disbelieve her. I'm just exercising a rational level of scepticism. She has a motive, sort of. And no alibi."

"Would take a bit of luck, that. How would she know he'd be alone?"

"Maybe he told her. Maybe he'd said he wanted some time to himself. For all we know, she'd arranged to meet him in private."

They returned to the living room. Helena Whiteside got steadily drunker and less communicative as the minutes drifted by.

"Okay if I leave you here?" asked the sarge after half an hour.

"Fine by me," said Nina.

Helena shrugged.

For nearly an hour after that, Nina tried to engage the woman in conversation. Helena had only started drinking when the truth had come out about her husband's past. Up till then, despite being a widow for just forty-eight hours, she'd been content with tea.

"Reckon you can go," said Helena, finally.

"I think I should stay," Nina replied. "You don't want to be alone if those men come back."

"They won't be coming back."

"How do you know?"

Helena just nodded, as if that were an answer.

Nina tried again a few minutes later. "Is there anything I can get you, Helena? Something to eat, maybe?"

"You can go."

"I really—"

"Look, it's still my house, isn't it?"

"Yes, but—"

"And if I don't want you here, you can't stay, right?"

"Well, yes, but I don't—"

"Look..." Helena paused, her eyes glazed now, attempting to focus on Nina. "Naomi, wasn't it?"

"Nina."

"Yeah. Same thing. Look, thanks and all that, but really, I want to be by myself. I'm not worried about those lads. Just, you know, bugger off, okay?"

Nina stood. There was nothing she could do about it. If Helena wanted her out, she'd have to go.

"If you change your mind—"

"I won't change my mind."

"If you change your mind," Nina continued, "call me."

She dropped her card on the table by the near-empty bottle and walked away.

CHAPTER THIRTEEN

"Strange day." Zoe kicked off her shoes and threw herself onto a kitchen chair. Yoda looked up at her from the counter.

"Strange how?" Carl was still in his suit, the one with the faint pinstripe lines that he'd bought before they'd moved up from Birmingham.

She narrowed her eyes. He still looked good in that suit. When had she stopped noticing things like that?

"What?"

"Sorry. I was miles away. We've got a new case."

"Murder?"

She nodded.

"I haven't heard about it." He slipped out of his jacket and opened the fridge. He handed her a can of fizzy lemon water without asking.

"It's not like you hear about all my cases, is it?" she asked.

"I suppose not, no. It's just, well. Murder. Usually makes the news."

He grinned at her and took a swig from his beer. The cat mewed.

"Yeah, that's the thing. It won't have been on the news. I spent most of today thinking Chris had made a mistake and it was an accident. But now..."

"Now what?" He pulled out the chair opposite her and sat.

"Things just got a bit complicated. That's all."

She forced a smile and asked whether he'd decided what they were having for dinner. She'd have asked him about his day, but she knew what the answer would be: he couldn't tell her.

And maybe he wouldn't, even if he could. She'd kept things from him, after all. She'd kept quiet about her contact with David Randle for over a year until he'd found out. He hadn't said anything, even after she'd apologised. He'd just waved the apology away, said it didn't matter now.

He stood up and got something else out of the fridge. A stew he'd made over the weekend.

It's a bit hot for a stew, she thought. But he'd made it. Zoe wasn't going to complain. She finished her drink and went to feed the cat. She bent down and spoke to him. He ignored her.

Everything lately seemed to be about work. She couldn't get it off her mind, either the cases she was working, or Streeting and Carter, or Fiona and the IOPC investigation. Not to mention David Randle and Olivia Bagsby, and Elena, and the women they'd rescued from the warehouse in Workington. There'd been a sense, back when they'd found the gun that had killed Bobby Silver, and Olivia had escaped Carter's last attempt to silence her, that things were finally coming together.

But that had been nearly half a year ago. Since then, things had just drifted.

She couldn't go on like this. Something would have to change.

CHAPTER FOURTEEN

AARON WAS through the second-to-last set of double doors when he heard the voice calling him.

"Sir!"

He ignored her and carried on. Just the rest of this corridor, then round the corner to the final door. She wouldn't follow him that far. The people here were too busy to waste time chasing people through corridors.

"Sir!" she called again. "You can't be in here. I'm sorry."

He sighed and stopped, rolling his eyes before he turned to face her. It wasn't her fault. She was just doing her job.

She was closer than he'd expected. Fast, then. And silent. One of those brisk, no-nonsense nurses that seemed to keep the place running. Young, but not nervous.

"I'm terribly sorry," she said. "But visiting hours ended quite some time ago. I'm afraid you'll have to come back..."

She frowned and took a step closer, eyes on the warrant card he'd just produced. It was a low trick, and not a particularly honest one, since he wasn't actually in the hospital on police business. The old Aaron Keyes would have been appalled. Denise wouldn't mind, he reckoned.

He found himself reevaluating that assessment five minutes later when he told her about it.

"As long as you don't get caught, Aaron."

"She's not exactly going to—"

"It's a slippery slope, is all I'm saying."

"It's just visiting a friend in hospital, Denise. It's not like it's—"

"It's a slippery slope, Aaron. One day you're flashing your warrant card when you shouldn't be, next thing you know, you're tipping off gangsters and springing murderers from court transports."

"I don't think..." He stopped.

She was shaking. Lying there on her hospital bed, scarred, and shaking.

She was laughing at him.

"Very funny. How are you feeling?"

"Good. They tell me I can go home in the next few days."

"Is your house...?"

"The house is fine. I can walk. I might need a few rails to drag myself around when I get tired, for the first week or two, but that's some other sod's problem."

The police would have to take care of that. But from what he knew of Denise, she wouldn't use those rails, even if they were there.

"Walk?"

"Yeah, why not?"

The walk in question took them out through the same sets of doors and past the nurse he'd pulled his warrant card on, who now stared at Aaron with the look of someone who realised they'd been had. Down two flights of stairs, slowly and carefully – Denise wouldn't take the lift – and out into the open air.

"Ah, the sweet scent of the outdoors." She lifted her head and sniffed.

The scent in question was mostly exhaust fumes from the cars circling the West Cumberland Hospital, looking for somewhere to park, but even that was probably better than being stuck inside all day.

She was moving well, now.

It was difficult to believe this was the same woman who'd come so close to death. The same woman who'd lain in an induced coma for weeks, who, when she'd finally opened her eyes, had been told she'd never speak again, then that she'd never walk again, and finally that she'd never work again.

They should have known better. She'd be returning to limited duties within the next few weeks.

It took more than a car bomb to take Denise Gaskill out.

He spent a few minutes with her back in her room. The place was packed with fresh flowers, despite Denise telling everyone who visited her that flowers weren't really her thing.

He checked over the labels. Senior cops, most of them. People who'd have had their secretaries diarise it and then actually do it, once a month, flowers to that PSD woman who got herself blown up. A couple of names he didn't recognise. One elegant green vase filled with roses, chrysanthemums, and others he didn't recognise. Looked expensive. No name on that one; no label at all.

"Secret admirer?" he asked.

"One of many," she replied.

"Shit." He checked his watch. "Got to go."

He hadn't noticed the time. Serge had promised him a

slap-up meal – home cooking, but Serge was one hell of a cook. Annabel would be staying up to join them, for the first part of the evening, at least. As he made his way back out, he found himself inhaling the way Denise had, sniffing the air, not caring about the fumes.

Denise was going home, summer was on its way, and things were going well at work and at home. Best enjoy it while he could.

CHAPTER FIFTEEN

"Right," Zoe said. "Let's go through what we've got. Nina, want to kick things off?"

They were in the team room, Nina, Tom, and Zoe. Another hot day, another cloudless sky. The national press muttered about drought.

No chance of that up here. Not after the six months they'd just had.

"Right." Nina stood. "Pete Whiteside, formerly Richard Black. Of the people who were with him on the trip, we've had cooperation from everyone except Gregory Howgill."

"Arsehole," said Tom.

"I beg your pardon?" Nina frowned.

"Not you. I mean Gregory Howgill. Wouldn't even provide prints and DNA."

"Not that we've got anything to compare them to," Zoe pointed out.

"Right, then." Nina continued. "Gregory Howgill. No prints or DNA, but no motive, either, and no indication that he left the rest of the group at any point."

"Same goes for the rest of them, though," Tom said. "They were all together. Except the couple. And they were with each other."

"Yes." Zoe stood, went to the board, and stared at the names for a moment. "And one half of that couple works at the Port of Workington. What was he like?"

"Nervous," said Nina.

"Same for Bella," offered Tom. "But they've got reason, haven't they?"

"True," agreed Zoe. "But still. I've sent Aaron over to have a word with Liam."

"Why?" asked Nina. "I think I got what I could out of him, boss."

"I'm sure you did. But where the port is concerned, you can't take anything at face value. What else have we got?"

"There's the wife. Helena Whiteside. No alibi, she was planning on leaving him, and she'd recently found out he'd been lying to her about his past. Sort of a motive there, but not much opportunity."

"Agreed. We need to keep her in mind."

"And then there's the people Pete owed money to."

"But why would they kill him?" Tom asked. "Beat him up a bit, maybe. But killing him doesn't make it easier to get their money."

"Maybe that was the plan," Nina said. "Rough him up. Got out of hand. Or maybe they're sending a message to other people who owe them money."

"Hell of a message."

Zoe watched the back-and-forth with a smile. They were a good team. Tom turned back to his screen, checking through the team inbox. He was good at this. Making sure nothing had been missed. Slotting the pieces into place. And

Nina – hard to see in her the woman she'd been a year and a half ago. The reckless DC, desperate to prove herself, slipping up all over the place, hoping her triumphs outweighed her defeats.

Losing them? Leaving them?

Where had that thought come from?

"Boss?"

She blinked. They were watching her.

"What?"

"Aaron's at the Port?" Tom asked.

"Yes. Why?"

Tom tapped his screen. Nina was already standing by his desk.

Zoe approached. "I reckon he might want to see this."

CHAPTER SIXTEEN

"Look, I don't know what you want me to say. We were together the whole time. Me and Bella. You trying to fit me up or something?"

"Okay." Aaron took a breath. "Let's take a break, shall we?"

"Fine." Liam stubbed out his cigarette and slipped it into his pocket. "I need to get back to work anyway."

Aaron watched as he walked back to join the rest of the shift. Miles separated himself and ambled over to where Aaron stood, behind a shipping container that provided privacy and shelter from the blazing sun.

"Get anywhere?" Miles asked.

Aaron shook his head. "What do you reckon of him?"

"How d'you want me to answer that?" Miles shot back. "If I back him up and I'm wrong, will you come after me?"

"No. I just want your opinion. You know him, I don't."

"He's a decent lad. Not the hardest worker, but not the worst, either. He's honest, though."

"You're sure of that?"

"I wouldn't swear it on oath. But if you're looking for a murderer—"

"How d'you know we're looking for a murderer?" Aaron asked.

Miles laughed. "Aaron, when aren't you looking for a murderer?"

"Fair point."

"Anyway, just my opinion. He's not a liar."

Miles walked back to his crew. Aaron took a breath. Miles' opinion was better than nothing, but what would he know? He'd been close with Bobby Silver, and hadn't seen anything amiss there.

None of them had.

"Bugger off," he heard from behind him. He wheeled around in surprise to find himself face to face with Stacey. Another one from the same shift. Another old friend of Bobby's.

But it wasn't Stacey who had spoken.

"Wipe your feet," said Bobby's old parrot, its head turned to the side, one eye staring at Aaron.

Freddie wasn't a small bird, which meant it wasn't a small cage. Stacey held it up from the ground and away from her body to prevent it tangling with her earrings.

"Want a hand with that?" Aaron asked.

"You're alright, DS Keyes."

DS Keyes, still. It had been Aaron for a while, the four of them having the occasional drink at the Henry Bessemer. Now one of them was dead, and another was calling him DS Keyes. At least Miles still called him Aaron.

His phone buzzed. A message from Tom, with a picture attached. Aaron opened it as Stacey walked away. He reread the words, checked the photo again, and took a long, slow breath before emerging from the shade of the shipping container and approaching the crew.

Not a liar, eh?

In that case, why was Aaron looking at a time-stamped photo that showed Liam in the distant background, clearly alone, during a period when he'd insisted he was with Bella the whole time?

Two minutes and one disgruntled Miles later, Liam was back behind the container with him.

"What is it now?" he asked.

"I'm going to have to caution you," Aaron told him.

Liam took a step back. "What? Why?"

"Save it for the station, Liam."

"Am I under arrest?"

"Not yet."

"Do I have to come?"

"No." Aaron turned and started to walk away. "But if you don't, things won't go well for you."

"Fuck's sake," said Liam, falling into step behind him.

CHAPTER SEVENTEEN

IT WAS FUNNY, the way these investigations progressed.

This one had started in the picturesque surroundings of the Hardknott Pass. Nina hadn't been, but she'd seen the photos. Tongue Pot. Esk Falls. Spectacular, even for someone used to the wonders of the Lake District.

And now it was taking her to a row of body shops just off the main drag in Distington. She opened the passenger door – they were in a patrol car, with Roddy the designated driver – and inhaled.

Salt, fish, and motor oil.

There were no clear suspects for the Whiteside murder, although the lad Aaron was bringing in might end up being one. But at least they knew who all the players were. All except one: the person, or group, who'd come after Pete for his gambling debts. They had no name and no contact details. But they did have the licence plate for the shiny black BMW, and that licence plate had led them here.

The registered owner was a Warwick Jones. There was nothing about Warwick Jones on the system: a broader search produced photos of a man in his fifties or early sixties, bald, smiling. Definitely not one of the twins the sarge had seen outside the Whiteside house. There was nothing else. The address, the photo, and no other information at all.

Warwick Jones appeared harmless enough, but with Aaron's description of the twins, Nina was glad she had Roddy with her.

She'd just swung one leg out of the car when her phone rang. She didn't recognise the number, and was considering letting it drop, when Roddy raised an eyebrow at her and she answered.

"Is that Naomi?"

"No," she said. "It's—"

"Sorry. I mean Nina. I've got your card here. Least, I managed to read the number right." Helena Whiteside gave what sounded like a nervous laugh. "Look, I'm sorry if I was rude last night."

"Don't worry about it," Nina said. "You've been through a lot."

She waited. Whatever Helena Whiteside had called her for, it wasn't to apologise for kicking her out.

"The thing is," Helena continued, "I should have been a bit more honest with you."

Here it came.

"You and the other one. Aaron. I told him there wasn't another bloke."

Roddy had slid back into the driver's seat. This time the silence went on so long, Nina had to speak.

"Are you saying you've been seeing another man, Mrs Whiteside?"

"Yes. Look, it's not what you think. I mean, Pete didn't know, and I would have left him anyway. None of this has anything to do with what happened to him. But it occurred to me that, you know, you might think I was involved or something, and I didn't have an alibi. Well, truth is, I do."

"You were with this other man?"

"Yeah," said Helena. "All day. And look, that's kind of why I asked you to leave yesterday. I wanted Gary over with me. I'd called him earlier. He'd said he was coming, and I thought, it wouldn't look right if he showed up and you were there. And then those men – I wasn't worried about them."

Nina glanced ahead and over the road, at the small building – little more than a garage – that was their destination. There was a patch of ground that seemed to serve as a car park round the back, and she could see the edge of a black vehicle. Possibly the BMW. They'd know soon enough.

"You weren't worried because you planned on having this Gary with you?"

"That's right. They wouldn't mess..." She stopped, then started again. "Anyway, I spoke to Gary, and he said I should come clean."

"He's right. We'll need to talk to you again, but in the meantime, can you give me Gary's full name and contact information?"

Nina put the phone to her shoulder and felt around for a pen and paper, then looked to her right to see Roddy holding them out for her. She noted down the details.

"Thanks, Mrs Whiteside. I'll need to check this out. We'll be in touch."

Forget Liam at the Port of Workington. Nina couldn't help feeling that Helena, Gary, and the mysterious Warwick Jones were where the action was.

CHAPTER EIGHTEEN

BELLA FRITHSDEN HAD TAKEN some convincing on the phone. But the suggestion that Tom could call the head and smooth things out himself had done the trick. She was here, just an hour after Tom had found the photo that showed she and Liam had been lying.

Here, in Interview Room Four. Under caution.

She'd been reminded of her right to a lawyer. She'd opened her mouth, then closed it, then opened it again. "Do you think I need one?"

"That's up to you," Tom said. "We can't advise you either way. All we can do is ask you to tell us the truth, Bella. A man's been murdered. We want to find out who did it."

The boss nodded approvingly.

There was no lawyer. Just the three of them.

"How well do you know Liam Cunliffe?" Tom asked.

"What?"

"He's your boyfriend, isn't he?"

"Yes. What's this got to do with him?"

"How well do you know him?"

She turned to look at the boss, who just looked back at her.

"I don't know," she said. "Quite well, I suppose?"

"How long have you been together?" asked the boss.

Bella turned back to look at Tom. "I don't know."

"You don't know?" DI Finch echoed.

"I mean, yes, of course I do. Six months. What... You don't think Liam did this, do you?"

"Why?" Tom asked. "Is there reason to think he did it?"

Bella shook her head.

Tom had wondered whether there was some sort of coercion going on. Whether Liam had killed Pete Whiteside and forced Bella to back him up. But if she'd been lying to them, then she hadn't done it out of fear. Either she believed Liam was innocent, or she loved him enough not to care.

And talking of lying...

"Why did you lie to us?" asked the boss. Her voice was gentle.

"What... What do you mean?" Bella replied.

"A man's been murdered, Bella," Tom said. "And in the course of our investigation, you've lied to us. You insisted that you and Liam had been together the whole time you were out at Tongue Pot and the other pools. The whole day."

"Yes?" said Bella.

Tom slid the photograph across the desk. "This photo shows Liam at Tongue Pot. Alone."

"Oh," said Bella.

"Do you want to—" Tom began.

"It's not him," she said.

"Are you saying that's not Liam Cunliffe? In the photograph?"

"No, not that. It's Liam in the photo. I mean, it's not Liam that killed Pete. Someone else did it. It can't be Liam."

"Why not?"

"Because... Because he wouldn't. He just wouldn't."

"Bella," said the boss, "both you and Liam have insisted you were together the whole time. We've just shown you a photo of Liam that proves you weren't. You've been caught lying to the police in the course of a murder investigation. The least you can do is tell us why."

There was a pause.

"Fine," said Bella. "Look, it wasn't his idea. It was mine."

"What was?" Tom asked.

"Lying," she replied. "I mean, yes, we weren't together the whole time. He said he wanted to see one of the other pools, but I was too tired for the extra walk. It was only for a few minutes. Your photo, it must be that. Him heading off."

"Why lie about it?" asked the boss.

"Look, I know how it works. I'm female, I'm a teacher, a professional, I'm in the clear."

Tom frowned.

"Not in the clear," she clarified. "But you'll have certain expectations. You won't just assume I'm guilty because of what I look like or where I work. It's different for him. Young working-class male. Works at the Port of Workington. I know the way you lot think. You'll assume it's him, and you'll..."

"We'll what, Bella?" asked the boss. "All we'll do is investigate this crime, thoroughly but fairly. If you think we—"

"Not *you*. I mean you the police, not *you* you. So I told him, we have to tell the police we were together. Either that, or they'll assume it was you. And I was right, wasn't I?"

"At the moment," Tom said, "we're just trying to piece together precisely what happened. Part of that involves getting the truth of who was where that day. If we're spending additional time looking into you and Liam, that's *because* you lied to us, not in spite of it."

She lifted her hands, palms out. "I think I've said enough."

CHAPTER NINETEEN

WARWICK JONES WAS SHORTER than Nina had expected, but that might have been the effect of the two men standing behind him. Seven feet tall, if she was any judge. And the sarge had been right; his companions were twins. Identical other than the broken nose.

"Mr Jones," she said as he stood in the open doorway.

He cocked his head. "Ah, the police."

She frowned – *how did he know?* – then she remembered Roddy Chen was standing behind her in his uniform. Her own giant.

"Come in." He turned away, the two companions shuffling to one side to let her and Roddy through. With the three huge men in the narrow corridor, the space was full.

She followed him to a kitchenette, two mugs on the table. The twins sat down and started to drink from them. They could have fit those things inside their mouths whole.

Don't stare.

"Up," Warwick Jones said, and the men stood. He took one of the chairs and gestured for her to sit opposite him.

The two men flanked him, Roddy behind her. Battle of the silent giants.

Or some kind of gangster summit. Nina stifled a smile.

He leaned back, giving her a broad smile which didn't make her feel at ease. "Call me Warwick." The smile widened. "I assume this is about the late Pete Whiteside."

"It is, yes," she replied. "What can you tell me about him?"

"We didn't kill him, I can tell you that. Right, lads?"

The two men either side of Warwick nodded.

"Didn't even know he was dead till your... What was his name?"

"DS Keyes," said one of the giants in a surprisingly high-pitched voice. Nina was surprised by the use of the sarge's rank.

"We didn't know he was dead till DS Keyes told Stu and Stevie here," Warwick said.

"And you really don't—"

Warwick cleared his throat. "The fact is, DC Kapoor..."

She wasn't going to tell him to call her 'Nina'. After a moment, he pursed his lips briefly and went on.

"The fact is, we operate in the sort of business where people can get the wrong idea," he said. "Where you, the police, that is, can make assumptions about our business practices. Assumptions which, as often as not, are far from the truth. So let me set you straight. We didn't kill Pete Whiteside. We're not in the habit of killing our customers. It's not good for business."

Which was exactly what they'd already guessed back in the team room. Killing off the debtors didn't pay well. But there were still other possibilities. All plausible enough.

Probably better to have that conversation back at the

Hub, under caution. But Nina had the feeling they'd decline her invitation. She had no cause to arrest them. And she didn't think they'd fit in the car, anyway. Might as well throw down here.

"What about an accident?" she asked, and he frowned. "If there had been a simple conversation that got out of hand, maybe a mistake was made, well, in those circumstances, we wouldn't necessarily be looking at murder."

He nodded. He'd understood the point she was making, at least. He sat forward and spoke slowly, enunciating each word clearly, so there was no danger of misinterpretation.

"We don't make mistakes, DC Kapoor."

Fair enough. She'd given them a chance, at least.

"What about Helena Whiteside?" she asked.

Warwick Jones smiled and sat back in his chair.

"We've decided not to pursue the estate of the deceased any further."

"Why not?" she asked, and to her surprise, it was one of the giants who replied.

"We're not gonna mess with—" he began, then stopped at a glare from his boss.

Warwick Jones was still smiling.

"A gesture of sympathy," he said. "Towards a grieving widow. Now, is there anything else?"

There was nothing else. She thanked them for their tea and candour and left, Roddy following silently behind.

Warwick Jones and his giants hadn't killed Pete Whiteside. She was convinced of that.

But she'd heard something else. Something that piqued her interest. Something that was definitely worth following up on.

CHAPTER TWENTY

NINA WAS OUT CHASING LEADS. The sarge was stuck in traffic on the way back from Workington. The boss had marched from the Beth Frithsden interview to her office to deal with paperwork. The look on her face was enough to convince Tom not to try for promotion, ever. Nina could climb the ranks, deal with admin and budgets and politics and people. Tom would stick to catching criminals.

And now it was quiet in the team room. Just the way he liked it.

They'd got as far as they could with Bella. She'd agreed to stick around, but she'd be wanting a lawyer now, which was fine. She'd let more than enough slip. Liam Cunliffe wouldn't be back for another few minutes, which meant a few minutes finding out what they could about him.

Tom got to work.

Five minutes later, he paused and looked around the room. Still no one here. No footsteps outside. No updates on his phone. And nothing on Liam Cunliffe.

It wasn't just their systems. It wasn't just that the man

he'd spoken to at the Port of Workington had told him to "Fuck off and come back when you've got a warrant."

It was the whole internet. You'd think a bloke in his twenties would be all over social media, but Liam Cunliffe was conspicuous by his absence. He could be running his accounts under a pseudonym. Tom did that, for his Instagram and YouTube, but Tom had good reason to. Even the reverse image searches came out blank.

He tracked down Bella's Facebook account, hoping to find something there, but apart from old Candy Crush updates, there were just a handful of serious posts about the state of the education system.

Maybe she had a separate account, too. Maybe they both did.

He spent another five minutes delving through nooks of the web that most people didn't know existed. He sat scratching his head and wondering why they hadn't just accepted her explanation and let her go.

She'd lied. They'd both lied. But they'd done it to protect Liam, from...

From what?

That line she'd used. "Young working-class male." It was true, Liam was a young working-class male, which attracted its own sort of trouble, especially from the police.

But on her lips, it had sounded like a line.

He switched focus, looking into Bella Frithsden herself. The first step would be to check out her employment history. He reached for his phone, paused, then remembered that the staff at Woodville Primary knew she wasn't around. They knew the police were involved, too.

He wasn't Nina. He could be subtle. He could tread carefully.

"Hello, this is DC Tom Willis from Cumbria CID. I'd like to speak to the head teacher, please."

"Ooh, is this about Bella?" said a female voice.

"It's just a routine enquiry."

"It *is* Bella, isn't it? Is she in trouble? You can tell me, DC Willis. In fact, it's probably best if I know."

"Is the head available?"

"Fine."

The line went dead. Tom stared at his phone for a few seconds before he realised it was talking to him.

Not dead, then. Just transferred, passive-aggressive style.

"Hello?"

"Ah, right. This is Mrs Albert. How can I help you?"

"I was just hoping for a little background about Bella Frithsden."

"Mmmm," she repeated.

"Nothing sensitive. Just the basics. Like when she started, where she came from, that sort of thing."

"Mmmm," she repeated.

He'd had enough of these people. If they weren't digging for information, they were hoarding it like dragons. He opened his mouth to say something more assertive, possibly something rude, then stopped.

These people were the public. They could be as annoying as they chose to be.

"How is Bella? I hope you're treating her well," said Mrs Albert.

"She's fine, thank you. Being very helpful."

"Well, then. Basic information, you say?"

"If you don't mind."

"Wait a moment."

The line went silent again, but this time Tom kept his

phone pressed to his ear. She was back two minutes later with the details.

"She moved here eight months ago," she said, which tallied with what Bella had told them. "From London. I have the contact details for her previous school, if you'd like."

The public. Sometimes, they gave him what he wanted.

CHAPTER TWENTY-ONE

GARY PERKINS WORKED IN PARTON, on a side road off a side road Nina hadn't known existed until she directed Roddy down it, following her phone. Parton had a Main Street, which amused Nina, given how small the place was. Gary Perkins' workplace was somewhere between that and the actual main street, the road between Whitehaven and Workington. Nina could hear the sea through the open window, but as they drew up, it remained out of sight.

Parton was on the way back from Distington, if she didn't mind a bit of extra traffic. And something one of those giants had said – Stevie, or Stu, she hadn't known which – had intrigued her. When she'd asked why Warwick Jones had decided not to go after Helena White-side for her husband's debts, it had been the giant that had spoken.

"We're not gonna mess with—" he'd said, before his boss had shut him up.

Not gonna mess with—

He hadn't had the chance to say who they weren't going

to mess with, but Nina had a good idea. She'd heard the same words just a few minutes earlier, after all.

"They wouldn't mess..." Helena Whiteside had said. She, too, had stopped before she'd finished the sentence, but it had come in the middle of their conversation about Gary Perkins.

If he was enough to deter Stevie and Stu, Gary Perkins was worth dropping in on. It helped that Nina had Roddy with her. Just in case things got physical.

The address Helena had given her led them past a potholed yard with five cars in it, two of them up on blocks, to a building that looked like a cross between a small warehouse and a large shed. The paint was peeling on the window frames and the huge wooden double doors, and it looked like one good kick would send it all into the Irish Sea. If it hadn't been for the music pumping out through the walls, Nina would have assumed the place was derelict.

As Nina approached, Roddy one silent step behind her, she saw something written above the door, the grey letters scoured into paint a slightly different shade of grey. Probably some other colour originally, but wind and salt had that effect.

Waggoners Gym, it said.

She pushed the doors open and found herself in a dark, cavernous space, a roped-off area at its centre and racks of weights around the sides. The music was only slightly louder inside. A shirtless man in his twenties stood by the ropes, bending over a dumbbell. Even in the dark, Nina struggled to tear her eyes away from his physique.

Beside him was another man, closer to fifty, blonde, turning towards her at the creak of the doors, and looking at her out of one unblinking eye.

The other was covered by a patch.

"Can I help you?" he asked. His voice was soft but still somehow audible over the music.

"Yes," Nina said, then repeated it, louder. The older man tapped on his phone and the music was replaced by silence, shocking in its suddenness. "Sorry," she continued, although she wasn't sure why. "I was looking for Gary Perkins."

"And you are?" asked the man.

"Detective Constable Nina Kapoor. Cumbria CID."

She went to open her warrant card, but he waved it away.

"No need for that. We can talk in the back room. Marco," he added, turning to the younger man. "You carry on with that. Any problems, shout. Don't step up the weight without me here. OK?"

"OK," said the other man.

Nina followed Gary, assuming the man with the eye patch was indeed Gary, through the open space to a door she hadn't noticed, the reassuring presence of Roddy beside her.

She needed that. There was something about Gary's calmness that unnerved her.

Through the door was a small back room. Nowhere to sit. Just a small private space. Gary closed the door behind them and Nina almost felt the walls closing in.

Stop it. He's just some bloke. You've got Roddy with you.

But then, even the twins didn't want to mess with this particular bloke.

"You're Gary?" she asked.

He nodded. "This about Helena?"

Straight to business. That was good, at least.

"It is, yes. I was hoping you could—"

"Confirm I was with her the day Pete died? Yeah. I was. All day. Well, ten till about four. Had to get back here for a session."

Ten till about four more than covered the window during which Pete had died. *If* it was true.

"And last night?" Nina asked.

"I was with her last night, yeah. Why? Someone else get killed?"

"No," she replied, then wondered why. She didn't have to answer this man's questions.

He was still watching her out of that single eye. She hadn't seen it blink once.

"Right, then. Anything else?"

"No," she said, again. "Thank you."

She left without another word and didn't relax until Parton was disappearing in the rear-view mirror. Even then, the tension persisted as they sat in a traffic jam whose cause wasn't clear until they'd passed it: a truck by the side of the road, rear doors open, cans of paint smashed and emptying their contents all over the tarmac. Uniforms were on the scene already, but it wouldn't be clear for a while. And when it was, the road would be a headache-inducing combination of orange and green for weeks to come.

There was something about Gary Perkins that had her on edge. Something about the gym, the whole set-up. What was the *session* he'd had to get back for? Gyms had become one of the centres of the drugs trade, in Cumbria as much as anywhere else in England.

Was Gary running something like that, here? Something Pete had found out about?

She'd assumed that if there was anything pointing to

Gary Perkins, it would be the fact the man was having an affair with Pete's wife. But now, the possibilities had opened up.

CHAPTER TWENTY-TWO

"WELL, THAT WAS A WASTE OF TIME." The boss flung her bag on the table.

Aaron agreed. It had taken long enough to get back to the Hub, what with the paint incident outside Whitehaven. He'd tried to engage Liam in conversation, but the lad wasn't saying anything. In Interview Room Two, he'd declined a lawyer but repeated "No comment" to every question. At least he'd agreed to wait, in case they came up with more questions.

"We don't have enough to arrest him." Aaron pushed open the door to the team room. Tom was on his phone, jotting down notes. Nina was still out.

"No." DI Finch followed him in. "No motive, no physical evidence, just the fact that he lied about being with Bella the whole time."

"Got it." Tom put the phone down and stood. Excitement lit up his face.

"What?" DI Finch asked.

"He didn't give you anything?" Tom said.

"No." Aaron sat down heavily in his chair. Whatever Tom had, it wouldn't push this case further.

"Liam's not the only one who lied about their alibi," Tom said.

"What?" The boss frowned. "Oh, you mean Helena. Said she didn't have one, then said she did. Yeah. Nina's looking into that."

Tom shook his head. "No, I mean Bella herself. She said Liam had been with her the whole time."

"Yes?" Aaron's interest was piqued despite himself.

"Which means she said *she'd* been with *Liam* the whole time, too. And unlike Liam, Bella might have a connection with the victim."

Aaron sat up.

"Go on," said the boss.

"I've just been talking to her previous employer in London. She wasn't there long. Turned out she wasn't that keen on city life."

"Can't blame her," said Aaron.

The boss merely frowned. She still missed Birmingham, for all she claimed to be settled up here.

"That's not the point. The point is where she worked before that."

"Where?" asked Aaron and the boss simultaneously. The door opened and Nina walked in.

"Shoreham," Tom replied, wearing a look of triumph.

Aaron deflated. "Where's Shoreham?"

"Next door to Brighton," Nina replied.

"Exactly," Tom said. "The very place where, eleven years ago, Pete Whiteside, formerly Richard Black, was convicted of causing death by dangerous driving."

CHAPTER TWENTY-THREE

Tom grinned, looking around the room. He couldn't understand why they weren't as thrilled as him.

But it was a stretch, wasn't it? How many people were there in Shoreham, or Brighton, or both? And eleven years was a long time.

Still, it was more than they'd had. And if it hadn't been for what Nina was about to bring to the table, it might have been worth following up.

"Gary Perkins," she said.

Tom frowned. The boss looked blank. The sarge, who'd been nodding at Tom's revelation, turned to her.

"What about him?" he asked.

"Gary Perkins is Helena Whiteside's lover."

Back when they'd been rivals as much as friends, Nina might have enjoyed the disappointment on Tom's face. Now, she felt guilty.

But that wasn't enough to stop her.

"What?" said the boss.

"Are you sure?" said the sarge.

"She called me this morning," Nina said. "Said she was sorry she'd lied to us."

"Bloody hell," said the boss.

"Gary Perkins?" said the sarge.

Tom turned away, tapping on his keyboard, staring at his screen.

"So all of a sudden," Nina said, "Helena Whiteside has an alibi after all. Her lover. Except he's not just her alibi."

"No," agreed the boss. "I suppose he isn't."

The sarge frowned. Tom was focused on his screen. He coughed and looked round, then back again.

"He's her motive, too. The life insurance might not have been enough of a reason to take out Pete, but a lover on the side? And I've just been round and spoken to him. Reckon there might be more to Gary Perkins than meets the eye. If Pete found out about him, about the affair, whatever else he was up to—"

"Gary Perkins?" said the sarge.

"Reckon he might be dealing," Nina continued. "Or worse. I got a strong sense of something not being right at his place. Even the debt collectors seemed scared of him."

"What?" said the boss.

Tom coughed again.

"Warwick Jones. Says he's not going after Helena. Made out he was being generous, but one of his goons let something slip before he could shut the guy up. I got the feeling they didn't want to cross Gary."

"Gary Perkins?" said the sarge. "Really?"

Nina ignored him.

"Gary and Helena offer each other an alibi, but how do we know they didn't cook this whole thing up? She had a motive, she knew where Pete would be – it's posted on the group's public Facebook page. And now it turns out her only alibi is her lover, a man everyone seems terrified of."

"Gary Perkins from the old Waggoners Gym?" asked the sarge.

Nina turned to him.

"Yes, Sarge. Gary Perkins. The very same."

Tom cleared his throat. He'd turned and was looking at them now.

The sarge laughed.

"Yeah, you don't need to worry about Gary Perkins," he said.

"What?"

"Gary's one of the good guys. Gets kids off the streets and teaches them a bit of discipline at the gym."

"Come on, Aaron," said the boss. "'Teaches them a bit of discipline'? Really? I remember that one from Brum. Half the criminal gangs used to say the same thing. 'We're keeping them off the streets.' 'We're keeping them out of trouble.' And every time, these kids were just getting groomed for a very specific type of trouble. Did you see any girls at this gym, Nina?"

Nina shook her head.

Tom cleared his throat again.

"He trains girls, too," said the sarge. "You can pop downstairs and chat to a couple of them. I believe you know Martinez. She trained at Waggoners."

The room fell silent.

"I think Rob Collins had a spell there, too. I guess you could say they were being groomed for a very specific type of trouble, but at least they're on our side, right?"

"Two people," said the boss.

"You can't expect me to know everyone who's been

through that gym," said the sarge. "But if you want the details, speak to Morris Keane."

"Morris Keane?" echoed the boss.

Tom cleared his throat again.

"Do you need a Strepsil or something, Tom?" Nina asked.

"Morris Keane," confirmed the sarge. "Been best mates with Gary since they were kids. Gary sends the troublesome ones for a chat with Morris. Between the two of them, they usually sort them out. He still wearing that eyepatch?"

Nina nodded. She'd been meaning to ask about that.

"He's been wearing that for twenty years. Lost his eye saving Morris from a drunken mob. Bit of a hero, is Gary."

"Oh," said Nina.

Tom walked into the middle of the room. He cleared his throat, and shouted, "Oi!"

Three pairs of eyes turned to him.

"While you lot are jabbering about one-eyed men, I've got something."

"Why didn't you say?" asked Nina.

He shot her a look so full of venom she flinched.

CHAPTER TWENTY-FOUR

"Bella Frithsden." Tom looked around the room.

"You still on this Shoreham thing?" Nina's voice dripped with bitterness. Her grand idea had been spiked. Now she was out to do the same to him.

"Well, yes. It's a bit more solid than..." He stopped himself before he said 'Gary Perkins'. "I thought."

"Go on," said the boss.

"I've been going through her socials. Such as they are. Not a lot there, but they only came into existence a couple of years ago."

"That's no crime," Nina protested.

"No, it isn't. But it's suspicious. So I went back and looked over the records from the Richard Black incident. The dangerous driving."

He checked everyone was still with him.

"Black was seventeen, just passed his test, showing off for his sixteen-year-old girlfriend, Daisy Williams. Going too fast. Misjudged a corner, clipped a wall. Daisy's side of the car took all the impact. Richard walked away unhurt. He called 999, and paramedics were on the scene within minutes. But there was nothing anyone could do. Daisy died before they could get her out of the car."

He paused.

"And?" asked the sarge.

"I found some photos from the trial. Look."

He walked back to his desk, tapped an icon, and the images he'd tracked down appeared on the big screen. Three photos from outside court. The victim's family. He walked back to the screen and pointed to each face in turn.

"Mother, Mel Williams. Father, Ollie Williams."

He pointed to the girl standing between her parents.

"Sister. Jane Williams. Jane *Bella* Williams."

"Oh," said the boss.

"Blimey," said the sarge.

Nina was beaming. "Fucking hell."

"Richard Black wasn't the only person to change his name. Black's trial was eleven years ago. Ollie Williams committed suicide the following year. Mel Williams died from alcohol poisoning two years after that. Jane Williams went to live with her mum's sister, Alex Frithsden. She changed her surname to match theirs, adopted her middle name as her first name, and Bella Frithsden was born. She was thirteen when her sister was killed. And eleven years later, she was on the scene when the man who'd killed her died."

"Bloody brilliant, mate," said Nina.

The boss's phone rang. She listened and spoke for a few seconds, then ended the call.

"Well, the good news is that Bella's lawyer's turned up, so

we can put this to her and see what she has to say for herself."

"And the bad news?" asked Tom.

She pursed her lips. "It's Stan Basham."

CHAPTER TWENTY-FIVE

"We've got a motive, and we've proved the alibi's false. Enough to arrest?" Tom asked as they made their way downstairs.

"Let's see how we go." Zoe didn't want to dampen his spirits, and they probably had enough for an arrest, but she'd need more for a charge.

There was no physical evidence that Bella was involved. And a decent defence lawyer would argue that there hadn't been a killing at all. Chris was a good pathologist, and if he thought Pete Whiteside had been murdered, then Zoe would back him. But convincing a jury beyond reasonable doubt?

They needed more.

Bella Frithsden sat quietly, impassive, hardly moving as they entered. Beside her, Stan Basham stood, grinned, then sat back down without shaking hands or anything that a decent, normal human being might have done.

"Hello, Stan," said Zoe.

"I see you've brought one of your trained monkeys with

you," Basham replied. It had been months since she'd seen him, but he hadn't changed.

Tom frowned. He'd crossed swords with Basham enough times to know the rules. You played it straight. You didn't get drawn into anything. No excuses. No mistakes.

"No, really, DC Willis, I shouldn't have said that," Basham added.

Zoe looked up from her notes, surprised.

"I'm sorry," he continued.

"Are you?" asked Tom.

"Yes, I am. I shouldn't have assumed that you were trained." Basham grinned again.

Normal service had resumed.

Tom read the formalities, then jumped straight in.

"Bella, we've been doing some digging. You haven't been honest with us, have you?"

"Are you accusing my client of lying, DC Willis?" asked Basham.

Tom ignored him. "Leaving the false alibi to one side, you haven't disclosed your prior knowledge of Pete Whiteside. Richard Black, as he was known eleven years ago. Back when you were—"

"Yes, alright," said Bella.

"Alright?" echoed Tom.

"Alright. Yes. I knew him. He killed my sister. He went to prison. Not long enough, but at least he paid for it. He changed his name. A few years later, I changed my name, too. I didn't know he was in Cumbria when I moved up here. I didn't expect to see him in that bloody group."

Zoe turned to look at Tom. They'd expected more resistance. He opened his mouth to say something, but she kicked him gently under the table. Sometimes it made more sense to let them talk.

"I recognised him immediately. He hasn't changed, you know. And he'd stuck in my head. You can imagine. I was thirteen, he was my big sister's boyfriend, he had a car, I thought he was the coolest thing on earth. And then he killed her, and I thought there wasn't a bigger bastard on earth. So yeah, you could say I remembered him."

She stopped. Zoe waited, but Stan Basham was whispering to his client.

"Did he recognise you?" Zoe asked.

"No," said Bella. Basham shook his head, but she ignored him. "I was only his girlfriend's little sister, but after everything that happened, you'd have thought he'd know who I was. But no. Not a thing."

Zoe remembered the notes Aaron had taken from his interview with Helena, Whiteside's widow. Selfish, she'd called him. You'd have to be, not to remember Bella.

Time to move in.

"Did you kill him?" she asked.

"No," said Bella.

"Did you confront him, get into an argument, lose your temper?"

"No."

"Maybe he saw you as a threat, thought you'd expose him. Was that it?"

Basham looked up, surprised to see Zoe building his client's defence for him.

"No," said Bella. "Look, nothing happened. All this, it's just a coincidence."

"Pretty big coincidence," Tom observed.

"Not big enough to send my client to prison," Basham replied.

"I did nothing. Liam did nothing. We're young and in love and for some reason you think that means we're murderers."

Beside Zoe, Tom's mouth fell open. Across the table, Basham was grinning again.

"If I were you, I'd let this one go," he said. "I can't see you and the monkey cracking her. Not sure I even need to be here. But I get paid whatever the result, so I'm not complaining."

Zoe eyed him. "Short break," she said.

CHAPTER TWENTY-SIX

"I'd never fit anyone up," said Nina. "I want to make that clear."

The sarge turned away from the screen to stare at her.

"Right?" he said.

"But if I did fit someone up, it would be Stanley Basham."

"Ah."

The sarge nodded and turned back to the screen. DI Finch had paused the interview, which cut the feed automatically.

"How the hell are we going to get her talking?" Nina said, pointing at the blank screen.

"If anyone can do it, the boss can."

"What would Denise do?" she asked aloud.

The sarge snorted. "Probably something that would have DI Whaley pulling his hair out."

"True. But the boss would approve. *Our* boss."

She tapped the rewind button and ran through it again. The whole interview.

There wasn't a point of weakness.

Tom arrived, the boss behind him, both of them sighing in frustration. Nina hit rewind and watched it again as the others chatted quietly around her.

There.

There.

Nina paused, rewound a few seconds, played it again.

I did nothing. Liam did nothing. We're young and in love and for some reason you think that means we're murderers.

She paused again, gave it a moment, rewound, watched it a third time. Or was it a fourth?

"What is it?" asked Tom.

"Liam," she replied. "Why mention him? What's it got to do with him?"

"Nothing," said DI Finch. "They're in love. I'd imagine she's always thinking about him."

Nina couldn't imagine it herself. If her tone of voice was anything to go by, the boss was struggling too. But it rang true.

"Where's Liam?" Nina asked.

"They're moving him to Carlisle," Tom said. "There's a leak in the custody suite, apparently. Clive Moor's sorting it out."

Something caught at the edge of Nina's memory. Something she'd seen.

No. Not seen. She hadn't been there. She'd been somewhere else. Where? When? It was something she'd heard about, she thought. After it had happened.

After she'd got out.

The pieces slid into place. Mick Halfpenny. She'd been in the bastard's basement, trussed up in a bag. And the rest of them had been here, hammering on Mick Halfpenny and finding solid rock.

But Halfpenny's unwitting accomplices had been here too.

Nina stood, suddenly. Tom, who'd been next to her, took a step away.

"Boss," she said. "Mind if I have a crack at Bella Frithsden? With Tom?"

"Don't see why not," replied DI Finch. "Just try not to assault Basham. Not on camera, anyway."

Nina grinned. "Don't worry. Tom, give me five minutes. I just want a quick word with Clive."

CHAPTER TWENTY-SEVEN

"Fucking hell," said Stan Basham as Nina and Tom took their seats. "It's all monkey, no organ grinder."

Ignore it.

Tom glanced at Nina. She was smiling at the lawyer. She looked calm.

He read the formalities, and the interview recommenced.

"All coincidence, then. Is that right, Bella?"

"Yes."

"You're insisting you had nothing to do with the death of Pete Whiteside. I just want that clarified, for the recording."

There was a briskness to Nina's voice, a sense of getting things over with so she could carry on with other business. Tom saw the frown starting to form on Bella's face.

What other business?

He didn't know what Nina had up her sleeve, but whatever it was, Bella was rattled.

"Yes," Bella said after a short pause.

"You're sure of that?" Nina asked, looking not at Bella but down at the sheet of paper in front of her. It was blank, but Bella didn't know that. There was a file blocking her view. An empty file.

"Yes," Bella repeated, a hesitance in her voice that Tom hadn't heard before.

"It's just that our pathologist is sure he was murdered, and everyone's got an alibi except you and Liam."

There was a long silence. Nina looked up and stared Bella in the face.

"Is there a question here?" said Basham.

"Not really." Nina turned to Basham with a smile, a real, happy smile.

Tom could have sworn the lawyer blinked, a tiny double take.

"I just want to be sure," Nina continued, "that your client knows where she stands, where we stand, and, crucially, where Liam stands. Because yes, it's true." She turned back to Bella. "You're the one with the motive, not Liam, but then, as you've pointed out, on record, you're in love, the two of you."

"So?" said Bella, but the defiance failed to hide her fear.

"You recognised Pete Whiteside. You knew who he was, yes?"

"Yes. I've already told you that."

"You told Liam about it. He killed Pete."

"No—"

Nina ignored her. "You weren't together the whole time that day. We know this. We have the evidence."

"No, I didn't tell him—"

"Liam found Pete. Confronted him. Took him by surprise."

"No. He didn't know about Pete." Bella looked from one of them to the other, her head moving left to right and back again, desperation in her eyes and her voice. "Liam didn't know."

Nina fixed her with a sympathetic look.

"Why should we believe you when you lied about your alibi?" she asked.

"But I don't—"

"We don't know how it happened, whether Liam took him by surprise, or whether Pete knew something was coming. We'll have to run tests, full forensics, that sort of thing. I'm sure we'll find something."

"This isn't—"

"This way now, lad, don't make any trouble," said a loud voice from outside. Clive Moor. Custody Sergeant Clive Moor.

"But maybe he'll just tell us," Nina continued. "Maybe he'll make everyone's life easier."

"Come on, now, Liam," said Clive, his voice much louder than it needed to be, clearly audible through the door Nina had left ever-so-slightly ajar. Two pairs of footsteps marched by.

Bella's mouth fell open.

"He'll probably come clean, won't he?" Nina continued. "To protect you, I mean."

"No," said Bella.

Were those tears in her eyes?

"No, he won't?"

"No, I won't let him."

"Well, I don't see how you can stop him." Nina tilted her head to one side.

"I can if I—" Bella began, but Basham grabbed her shoulder and, when she turned to face him, mouthed the word, "No."

She shook him off and continued.

"I can if I admit it," she said.

"Admit what?" Tom asked.

"I did it," Bella said.

"You did what?"

"I killed him. I killed Pete. I told him who I was, what he'd done to my family. He said he was sorry, but he'd paid for it. Done his time. It was history."

"But not for you," Tom observed.

Bella shook her head. "I didn't plan it, you know? But I lost control, and I hit him, and he just stood there gaping at me like an idiot. He wasn't hurt. I needed to see him hurt."

"So you found a weapon?"

"I picked up a rock. I don't think he realised I was actually going to use it. But... He was down by the pool. I hit him hard, and he went straight down in the water."

Stan Basham put his head in his hands.

"Can I see him?" asked Bella.

"I'm sorry," said Nina. "He's not here."

"But..." Bella looked towards the door, frowning.

"He's not here," Nina repeated.

Basham lifted his head and fixed Nina with a stare that, to Tom's amazement, seemed to betray a grudging respect.

CHAPTER TWENTY-EIGHT

"Sɪᴛ ᴅᴏᴡɴ," said Fiona.

There was a scent in the super's office that reminded Zoe of something. Something familiar but out of place.

"Congratulations, Zoe."

Zoe opened her mouth for the usual routine: *it wasn't me, it was the team.* Even more true than usual this time.

But Fiona held up a hand to stop her. "You could have strung this one out a bit longer."

"I'm sorry?"

"How long since you had a decent case to sink your teeth into?"

Zoe frowned. There had been investigations. Small things that looked like they might grow into something larger, but then hadn't. Cases she'd handed back to local CID.

"January," she said.

Fiona nodded. "January. Bobby Silver and the one Aaron helped out with in Langdale."

Helped out with was a stretch. He'd solved the case, with

little help from anyone else. As she watched, Fiona took a sip of coffee from her mug and that familiar scent fell into place.

Canteen coffee. *Bad* coffee. There'd been no sign of Luke, Fiona's assistant, when Zoe approached her office. It looked like the super was slumming it.

Fiona must have seen the way her eyes lingered on the mug, because she shrugged.

"I'll miss him," she said.

"What?"

"Luke. He's gone for an interview."

"He's leaving?"

"If he gets it. It's a promotion, really. The Office of the Policy Advisor to the Assistant Chief Constable."

"Huh?"

"Becca Grey's office. He's interviewing to be her assistant. I can't stand in his way."

"Oh." Zoe felt strangely vulnerable without her own cup of coffee. Then she realised it wasn't lack of coffee that was the problem. It was what Fiona had just said.

Was Zoe standing in anyone's way? Was she standing in Aaron's way? Blocking Nina's path at the same time? And did they really *need* her here, running the team, with no big cases for months at a time?

"Anyway," said Fiona. "You've done good work. I gather she's going to plead loss of control. See if she can get it reduced to manslaughter."

"CPS will go for that, I reckon. Any news on—"

"Nothing," Fiona told her. "No news on the IOPC. No news on your friend Ralph Streeting, although I'm not sure they'd tell me if there was. Do you have any news for me?"

"No, sorry," said Zoe, without stopping to think about whether that was true. Fiona knew about Olivia, knew

Randle had been involved. She knew about the cache of emails that showed Carter had been directly involved in the negotiations to sell on the women he'd brought into Workington. And she knew they weren't enough to bring a charge.

"Fine, fine," said Fiona. She leaned back.

Zoe knew that look. *Dismissed.*

She went back to the team room, her feet dragging. They'd just got a result. And she was making progress, on Carter, and Streeting, and all of it.

Wasn't she?

She entered the team room, pulling on a smile. Nina was grinning, telling Aaron about the look on Stan Basham's face. Tom was holding up that godawful antimacassar, a question on his face. They turned to her, their smiles widening.

It would be fine. It would all work out.

Zoe would make sure it did.

CUMBRIA CRIME BOOK 7, THE PORT

With a long-term target finally in custody and the appearance of a key witness, DI Zoe Finch might have expected everything else to fall into place.

But when the body of a man she knows is found inside the Port of Workington, the investigation takes her team to some unexpected directions and working with some unlikely allies.

Why was he killed? Is there a connection with the missing mother of a local businessman? Can Zoe's team even keep the case in the face of a bitter territorial spat?

And as West Cumbria CID race to gather evidence before their prime suspect disappears, has her treated enemy finally slipped up?

Buy from book retailers.

READ THE CUMBRIA CRIME SERIES

The Harbour

The Mine

The Cairn

The Barn

The Lake

The Wood

The Port

...and more to come

Buy from book retailers.

ALSO BY RACHEL MCLEAN

The DI Zoe Finch Series – buy from book retailers.

Deadly Wishes

Deadly Choices

Deadly Desires

Deadly Terror

Deadly Reprisal

Deadly Fallout

Deadly Christmas

Deadly Origins, the FREE Zoe Finch prequel

The Dorset Crime Series – buy from book retailers.

The Corfe Castle Murders

The Clifftop Murders

The Island Murders

The Monument Murders

The Millionaire Murders

The Fossil Beach Murders

The Blue Pool Murders

The Lighthouse Murders

The Ghost Village Murders

The Poole Harbour Murders

The Chesil Beach Murders

...and more to come

The McBride & Tanner Series – buy from book retailers.

Blood and Money

Death and Poetry

Power and Treachery

Secrets and History

The London Cosy Mystery Series by Rachel McLean and Millie Ravensworth – Buy from book retailers.

Death at Westminster

Death in the West End

Death at Tower Bridge

Death on the Thames

Death at St Paul's Cathedral

Death at Abbey Road

The Lyme Regis Women's Swimming Club series by Rachel McLean and Millie Ravensworth – buy from book retailers.

The Lyme Regis Women's Swimming Club

A Brush with Death

The Mystery of the Runaway Reindeer

...and more to come

ALSO BY JOEL HAMES

The Sam Williams Series – Buy now in ebook, paperback and audiobook

Dead North

No One Will Hear

The Cold Years

The Art of Staying Dead

Victims, a Sam Williams novella

Caged, a Sam Williams short